Andrew's Robin

A family of robins live in Andrew's garden. When a squirrel causes some trouble, Andrew helps the robins, and later it is their turn to help Andrew.

Enid Blyton's

Andrew's Robin

illustrated by Edgar Hodges

Published in Great Britain by World International Publishing Limited,
An Egmont Company,
Egmont House, P.O.Box 111 Great Ducie Street, Manchester M60 3BL.
Printed in DDR. ISBN 0 7235 4449 2

A CIP catalogue record for this book is available from the British Library.

In Andrew's garden there was a little robin that he called his very own. It was a black-eyed, long-legged, red-breasted little bird, so tame that it would take a biscuit from Andrew's fingers.

That spring the robin had built its nest in an old saucepan under the hedge. Andrew remembered putting the saucepan there when he played house, and he had forgotten to take it away. The robin found it, and he and his little wife had put a cosy nest there.

Andrew was pleased. He watched the robins going to and fro from the nest. He saw the five eggs laid there. He even saw three of the eggs hatch out. That *was* exciting. The tiny birds inside the eggs pecked at the shell and broke it. Then out they came – bare black babies without a single feather on them.

The next day all five eggs had hatched. The robins threw the empty shells out of the saucepan nest, and began hunting for caterpillars and grubs to feed their five hungry babies.

"That will keep you busy," said Andrew, as he peeped at the five tiny birds, all with their beaks open. "When I dig my garden I will hunt for caterpillars too, and bring them to you."

One day a dreadful thing happened to the robins. A squirrel came that way and saw the nest in the saucepan. Now the squirrel liked, for a change, to make a meal of baby birds, so when he saw the little robins he ran over to them at once.

The father and mother were not there, as they had gone hunting for grubs. The squirrel picked up two of the tiny creatures in his mouth and ran off with them.

How those babies squeaked! The father and mother robin heard them at once and came flying back. When they saw the squirrel they knew quite well what he had been up to, and they flew at him, singing loudly in anger, for that is the way of robins.

The squirrel stopped. One robin flew at his right eye and the other flew at his left. He shook his head. He dodged. But it was no use. Those robins would not leave him alone until he dropped the baby birds.

So the squirrel dropped them on to the lawn, and then bounded off to a tree. Up he went and sat there making faces at the robins.

The robins flew down to their two frightened babies. They were not really hurt – but they could not possibly get back to the nest themselves. "We must carry them in our beaks," sang the mother robin. But alas! The babies were too heavy.

"Leave them, leave them!" sang the freckled thrush. "I don't bother about my young ones if they fall from the nest."

But the robins were not like the thrush. They would not leave their little ones. But what could they do? The babies were too heavy to carry.

"Fetch Andrew, fetch Andrew!" sang the father robin. "He is kind and strong."

So the robins went to fetch Andrew. He was in the playroom, building a big castle, and was very surprised to see the two robins fly in at the window.

The father robin flew to the top of Andrew's big castle and sang loudly to him. Andrew stared at him. The robin flew to the window and back again.

"What is it you want?" asked Andrew. The robin sang and flew to the window-sill. Andrew got up and went too – and he saw something on the lawn. What could it be?

He ran downstairs and out into the garden. As soon as he came to the baby birds, lying helpless on the grass, he guessed why the robins had come to him.

"They want me to put their babies back," said Andrew in delight. "Oh, the clever little things! They knew I would help them."

He gently lifted the two frightened baby birds and took them to the nest in the saucepan. He put them with the others and soon they settled down happily.

"Thank you!" sang the robins. "You are very kind!"

The robins were afraid of the squirrel after that. Always one of them stayed to guard the nest until the babies were too big to be taken away by a squirrel.

Soon they could fly. Soon they had flown. The little robin family split up, and they all left the garden, except the father robin. This little bird stayed there with Andrew, singing to him as he played in the garden. He never once forgot how kind the little boy had been to the baby birds.

One day Andrew took his clockwork train and lines on to the lawn. He set the train going and had a wonderful time with it. When it was tea-time he had to pack it up in a hurry and go in, and it wasn't till the next day that he found he had lost the key of his beautiful train.

"Oh, Mummy, now I can't play with my engine any more, because the key is lost," he said. "I have hunted everywhere in the garden, but I can't find it. I am so unhappy."

The robin heard him. He had seen Andrew winding up the engine. He guessed what the key was – that little shiny thing. He began to hunt for it.

At last he found it. No wonder Andrew couldn't see it, for it was halfway down a worm's burrow. The robin pulled it out. It was a bit rusty, but it was the lost key, there was no doubt about that.

The robin took it in his beak and flew to the playroom. He sat on the window-sill and made a little sound, for he couldn't sing very loudly with something in his beak. Andrew looked up.

"Oh!" he cried in delight. "You've found my key! You dear, good little bird! Thank you so very much!"

"You helped me, and I helped you!" sang the robin. "That is as it should be."

"Soon it will be winter-time, Andrew. Help me again and give me crumbs."

"I will, I will!" promised Andrew. And I know he will keep his promise.